W9-CEI-858

Theodor and Mr. Balbini
by Petra Mathers

Petra Mathers

Harper & Row, Publishers

Mr. Balbini had a dog. No wife, no children, no cat. Just Theodor.

When Mr. Balbini talked, Theodor sat on his hind legs and listened. He ate and slept when his master did. They went for walks.

Mr. Balbini was happy, and Theodor seemed happy too.

Then one day, at lunchtime, Theodor gave Mr. Balbini a funny look. "Beef Bits again?" he asked. "I've never been keen on Beef Bits."

Mr. Balbini was thunderstruck. His Theodor—a talking dog! His head buzzed with questions, but he couldn't get a word out. Finally he stammered, "Why, Theodor...I had no idea....Why didn't you speak up before?"

Theodor frowned. "Let's go for a walk," he said. "But no leash, please. And not down West Shore Road. I get tired of the same old streets, don't you? And the boathouse at the end of the block is a bore."

Mr. Balbini liked the same old streets. He especially liked the boat house at the end of the block. But he didn't dare say so.

It was drizzling outside. When they got home, they were soaked. "I don't like rain," complained Theodor, rolling on the rug. "Would you mind drying me off? I feel a bad cold coming on."

Mr. Balbini brought a towel. "A little more to the left, please," directed Theodor. When he was cozy, he curled up for his nap.

"What's for dinner?" he yawned.

Mr. Balbini had planned to have the last lamb chop and feed Theodor the rest of the Bow-Wow Beef Bits. But that was out of the question now. He opened the refrigerator.

"Macaroni and cheese?" he suggested.

"I don't think so," said Theodor.

"Chicken pie?"

"I wouldn't mind that last chop," said Theodor.

While Theodor rested, Mr. Balbini popped a chicken pie into the oven and fried the chop. He still couldn't believe what had happened. He shook his head and set the table for two.

After dinner, Mr. Balbini rushed to turn on the television. Every Sunday, he watched *Detectives from Outer Space*, his favorite program.

"But it's a rerun," snorted Theodor, who was snoozing on the sofa. "Wouldn't you rather watch *French Chefs*?"

Mr. Balbini sighed and switched to *French Chefs*.

"Turn it up a little, would you?" said Theodor, pricking up his ears.

Mr. Balbini suddenly felt very tired. He looked at his dog. "I could never call him old pooch again," he thought, and padded upstairs to his room.

"Too bad we don't have color TV," Theodor called after him.

Mr. Balbini slept poorly. He woke feeling tired and took a long shower. He wondered if Theodor was awake. It would be nice to have a quiet breakfast. He looked forward to reading the newspaper. He tiptoed downstairs.

Theodor was awake. He was already reading the paper.

"I want to learn French!" he announced, pointing to an ad:

MADAME POULET
French Without Toil

Mr. Balbini dialed the number. He explained to Madame that he had a very special student.

"All my students are special, Monsieur," she said, and promised to come that same day. "We shall start at the beginning, yes?" she asked when she saw Theodor.

During the lesson, Mr. Balbini retired to his armchair. The sun warmed the back of his head. His eyelids drooped. And he slept.

He dreamed of Theodor pushing a giant TV set around the house. On the screen was Madame Poulet, singing French recipes.

He woke with a start. Madame was smiling down at him. "Your Theo is so clever. He learns quick, quick. Please, let him visit me. I have many books he would like."

"Cookbooks," said Theodor.

"Yes," chuckled Madame, "and I am not such a bad cook myself."

Mr. Balbini was overjoyed. *"Peace and quiet,"* he thought. "My house will be my own again."

That afternoon, Mr. Balbini trimmed his rose-bush. He made some tea and read the paper. He started for his walk down West Shore Road to the boat-house at the end of the block. But he turned around.

It wasn't the same, walking by himself. The house seemed empty.

"I miss him," he said. "I miss the way he was *before* he talked."

Theodor called in the evening. "Madame has invited me to stay awhile. I hope you don't mind. We're having fun." Then Madame got on the phone.

"Oh, Monsieur, your Theo, he is so amusing! Why not join us for a little party tomorrow night? Then you can meet my Josephine."

The next evening, Mr. Balbini dressed with care. He wore his new hat and brought a bouquet of flowers.

Theodor opened the door. He was wearing a new hat too. But it was Josephine who looked glad to see Mr. Balbini.

"Let me show you my room," said Theodor, leading the way.

"Theo, come, help me whip the egg whites," Madame called from the kitchen.

Mr. Balbini was left alone with Josephine. He bent down to ruffle her ears. "What a good dog," he murmured. "Yes you are, oh yes you are."

Josephine snuggled closer. "And how do you like your new friend Theodor?" asked Mr. Balbini. Josephine frowned and gazed at him with damp eyes.

"I wonder," said Mr. Balbini. "Perhaps you would like to visit *me* for a while?"

Josephine wagged her tail. Mr. Balbini ran to the kitchen to ask Madame.

"Yes, *mais oui!* What a wonderful idea!" she said. Josephine barked, and bounced off to fetch her ball.

At dinner, Mr. Balbini and Madame discovered they both loved *Detectives from Outer Space.* "You know," she confessed, "I always watch it on Sundays, even though it's mostly reruns."

Mr. Balbini glanced down at Josephine and patted her nose. She licked his hand.

After the party, Josephine followed Mr. Balbini to his car. She hopped into the backseat.

"Why don't we all have a picnic next week?" Madame Poulet called as she and Theodor waved good-bye.

Mr. Balbini smiled as he drove off. "Tomorrow we'll take a nice long walk, Josephine," he said. "You'll love West Shore Road. And the boathouse at the end of the block."

For my one and only

Theodor and Mr. Balbini
Copyright © 1988 by Petra Mathers
Printed in the U.S.A. All rights reserved.

Library of Congress Cataloging-in-Publication Data

Mathers, Petra.
   Theodor and Mr. Balbini.

   Summary: Soon after the kindly Mr. Balbini discovers
that his dog, Theodor, can talk, he finds himself bullied
by the demanding canine and yearns for a more
traditional pet.
   [1. Dogs-Fiction.   2. Pets—Fiction]   I. Title.
II. Title: Theodor and Mr. Balbini.
PZ7.M4247Th 1988   [E]   87-45860
ISBN 0-06-024122-5
ISBN 0-06-024144-6 (lib. bdg.)

Typography by Constance Fogler
1   2   3   4   5   6   7   8   9   10
First Edition